Mt. Yonah

W ← → E
↓
S

Castle of the
Queen of the
BunnyBees

Kudzu

Entrance
to the
Cave

The Patch

GREAT
SWAMP

The
Great Rescue

Story by Kathleen N. Daly
Pictures by Jan Brett

One day the evil Lavendar McDade came up with a nasty plan to kidnap the critters that belonged to the Cabbage Patch Kids.

When no one was looking, she crept into the woods where she had often heard the Cabbage Patch Kids playing. With her were her evil companions, Cabbage Jack and Beau Weasel. Cleverly, they set out all kinds of tasty morsels. Then, as the critters were munching happily on the treats, Beau Weasel and Cabbage Jack rushed in and captured some of them.

When the 'Kids heard the news, there were tears in everyone's eyes. All the 'Kids gathered in the Castle of the Queen of the BunnyBees. It was a very sad moment.

"Which critters did Lavendar get her wicked hands on?" the Queen of the BunnyBees asked.

"I'll tell it out straight," said Colonel Casey, the wise old stork. "I can't rightly pretend it's not bad. Lavendar made off with Otis Lee's bulldog, Cap'n; Tyler Bo's chameleon, Dragon; and Cousin Cannon Lee's polka-dot pig, Pepper."

Everyone let out a sorrowful sigh. "But there's more," Colonel Casey went on. "You must save your sighs and tears 'til the end. Lavendar also got Dawson Glen's snake, Old Sneakers; Rebecca Ruby's turtle, Miss Myrtle; and Bobbie Jean's owl, Dr. Tee. Then there was Will Henry's frog, Popsicle; Ramie's hamster, Bun-Bun; and Baby Dodd's baby possum, Little Bitty. Nine critters in all."

"'ittle Bitty!" wailed Baby Dodd. "I wan' 'ittle Bitty!"

"We'll stop her," growled Cousin Cannon Lee. "We'll get our critters back if it's the last thing we do."

"Oh, Lavendar said you could get them back," said Colonel Casey. "All you 'Kids have to do is go to work for her in the gold mine. You know she needs lots of 'Kids to work there. She's as greedy for gold as a possum is for grubs."

"It's a trap," said Cousin Cannon Lee. "We could never trust her to set our critters free, even if we worked for her."

"We could try," said gentle Rebecca Ruby. "I would do anything to get back Miss Myrtle."

Otis Lee snorted, "She'll make us stay there for the rest of our lives, and keep our critters, too."

Will Henry stood up. "I have something to say."

Everyone hushed. Will Henry didn't talk a lot, but when he did, it was worth listening.

"I have a plan," said Will Henry. "We have to trick Lavendar worse than she tricked us. We'll do what she demands — go to work in the gold mine. Lavendar will think she has us for good. But my plan will free us and our critters, and put her in her place for a long time."

The 'Kids gave a loud cheer.

Will Henry looked pleased. "Now, listen carefully. I'm sure this plan can work."

Baby Dodd laughed. "Get 'ittle Bitty back!"

"Baby Dodd is too little to go," said Ramie.

"I go, I go!" protested Baby Dodd.

"Yes, he goes," said Will Henry. "That's part of my plan."

The Queen of the BunnyBees spoke: "I would feel better if Baby Dodd stayed here where he is safe. But I trust you, Will Henry."

"Good," Will Henry replied. "Now we must hurry and gather up all the balloons we can find and lots of firecrackers, and we must ask the BB-Bees to help."

"Take candy," commanded Baby Dodd.

"Okay," grinned Will Henry. "Bring your big bag of caramels, Baby Dodd. They'll be useful."

The 'Kids scurried around and gathered up dozens of balloons and firecrackers. Next the 'Kids put firecrackers and boxes full of hidden BB-Bees under the toys in Baby Dodd's toy box. They put the balloons under their clothes.

At the entrance to the mine, Lavendar lined up the 'Kids. "I've got you at last, you little brats!" she sneered. "You'll never get away. One problem from any of you, and it's goodbye and good riddance to your silly pets!"

"What's in that box?" Lavendar suddenly shouted, when she saw the big toy box.

"It has Baby Dodd's toys," said Ramie. "He's too little to work. We brought his toys to keep him out of trouble."

When Lavendar flung open the toy box, all she saw were toys, and Baby Dodd said to her, "Box of boom-booms. Go bang-bang!"

Lavendar slammed the box shut. "You silly 'Kid," she laughed. "Bang-bang! Boom-Booms!"

Cabbage Jack and Beau Weasel set the 'Kids to work at once. The gold mine was a dangerous place. There was so much dust in the air that the 'Kids could hardly breathe and there were big, dark holes that the 'Kids had to avoid. Their critters were with them, however, and that made the 'Kids feel somewhat better.

Lavendar worked them hard. The 'Kids pounded rock, hour after hour, sorting through it for pieces of gold. They were bone tired and scared. Only Baby Dodd was happy, because he had found Little Bitty. He spent his time talking to Little Bitty and feeding him caramels and saying, "'et's go home."

After days of hard work, Tyler Bo asked Otis Lee when they would put Will Henry's plan to work.

"Tonight we escape," whispered Otis Lee. "Will Henry and I have managed to tell everyone what to expect. We'll start when I give the signal."

"What will the signal be?" Tyler Bo asked Otis Lee.

"Baby Dodd is going to go up to Beau Weasel and say, 'Let's party!'"

Tyler Bo looked alarmed. He wondered what would stop Beau Weasel from hurting Baby Dodd and sending all of them back to work.

"That's where Dawson Glen comes in," said Otis Lee. "He has been told by Will Henry what to do."

Just then, Beau Weasel stared at them. Otis Lee whispered, "Wait for the signal, then follow my lead."

One hour went by, two hours, three hours. At last Will Henry whispered, "Come here, Baby Dodd."

Baby Dodd turned around and yelled as hard as he could, "'et's party!"

This startled Beau Weasel. He bared his teeth and looked ready to bite. But Dawson Glen went up to him and said, "We always work twice as hard after a party. We even have some balloons, if you'd like to see them."

Beau Weasel was suspicious, but he did want the 'Kids to work harder to find gold. "All right, I guess," he snarled, "but let me see one of those balloons."

While Beau Weasel examined the balloon every which-a-way, the 'Kids began to blow up the rest.

"Now wait one minute. I don't like..." Cabbage Jack began to say.

Baby Dodd toddled over to Cabbage Jack and Beau Weasel and offered them his bag of caramels. "Candy. Good," said Baby Dodd.

Cabbage Jack and Beau Weasel grabbed the caramels, and began to chew.

As soon as Cabbage Jack and Beau Weasel began to chew, their jaws stuck tight. They couldn't open them to holler or to bite. They knew that they had been tricked.

"Quick! The firecrackers!" commanded Otis Lee. "And let out the BB-Bees!"

The air was soon full of confusion. The 'Kids let their critters out of the cages. Otis Lee hollered, "Light the firecrackers! BB-Bees, shoot the balloons!" Beau Weasel and Cabbage Jack froze with terror.

Lavendar McDade came running to the entrance of the mine just as the 'Kids were running out.

It was an awesome sight! Firecrackers exploded. BB-Bees popped hundreds of balloons. Lavendar screeched and shrieked and the 'Kids ran as fast as they could away from the mine.

Lavendar and her nasty companions were furious.

"It's your fault," growled Cabbage Jack.

"No, it's yours," Beau Weasel snarled.

Back in the 'Patch, the exhausted 'Kids snuggled up with their critters and fell asleep, while the moon and stars kept watch through the peaceful night.

Blue Hole

The
Gold Mine

Kudzu

Lavendar's
House